Ja.....

The Mystery Beneath their
Feet

The Shoreline of Mysteries

About the Author

James Ford and his family spend the July 4th week in Ludington every year. James' father grew up in Ludington allowing for many family visits to the town as a child. James has a deep love for the city and even has gone as far as being a part of the 4th of July parade every year. Most of the things within this book are actually located within the town. At the same time, some things are made up. Figure it out and comment on James Ford's Instagram.

Follow James Ford on Instagram @AuthorJamesFord

"You never know until you try." - Jason
Pagaduan

Book cover designed by James Ford

ISBN: 9781686251450

Chapter One

The SS Spartan was officially launched into operation on January 4, 1952. It's home port, one of Michigan's most popular lakeside cities... Ludington.

However, secretly it was not the first time the Spartan had been used. The ship had been in operation for months before its official launch. It's first voyage on the Great Lakes was to participate in one of the largest gold smuggling operations known to man.

In 1951, the Spartan was secretly used for a trip from Escanaba, a small town in Michigan's Upper Peninsula, to Big Point Sable, a lighthouse located two miles north of Ludington State Park. It's cargo smuggled gold from Canada, valued at over five-hundred million dollars. The ship anchored two miles offshore. Eight fishing boats transported the stolen gold to Big Point Sable Lighthouse, where it would be loaded and trucked to a hidden location in the city.

My Name is Kane Winston, and I'm the only one to my knowledge that had witnessed what happened on that night.

That night, I followed the specious truck for as long as I could, but I couldn't keep up. I feared if I followed the driver too close he would spot me and become specious.

My friend Joe Windford lives on M116, the only road in and out of Ludington State Park. The following day I meet up with Joe and was telling him about what I had seen. At first, he didn't believe me. I started to tell Joe about the truck and how it had baby blue headlights, which seemed odd to me. It just so happened that Joe was sitting on his front porch looking at the stars that night. He too had also seen that same truck with odd blue headlights. Joe recalled also thinking it was odd, knowing that the State Park closes at 10PM. He knew it could only have come from one place... the State Park.

I knew something was not right with what we had seen. I jokingly said to Joe, "We need to get to the bottom of this. We might go down in the history books as the two famous crime fighting kids who saved the city of Ludington."

Joe chimed in, "We could be heroes. Maybe we could receive a reward from the government!"

Chapter Two

The following day, Joe and I went to the Old
Hamlin, a local diner on the avenue. It was a favorite
for many of the old timers and retires from Dow and
the Car Ferries. A group would meet up for
breakfast every morning. They seemed to know
everything that happened in our small town. We
talked to them for a couple of hours, seamingly
getting nowhere. Just before we left, a gentleman
about sixty-two with a white beard and wrinkled skin
walked in. He looked like he had just come in from the
beach with the amount of moisture dripping from his
face.

I walked up to him and asked him how his day
was going. He responded in his deep nasally voice,
"Not to bad; How about yourself?"

"Good, my name is Kane Winston and this is my friend Joe Windford. We have a couple of questions for you in regards to this town. Last night, my friend and I saw a semi-truck with blue headlights come from the state park after the park had already closed. I was actually at Big Point Sable Lighthouse last night and saw fishing boats load that truck up with big boxes.

The man stopped me in my tracks. "Are you kidding me, have you never heard of the legend of Big Point Sable? It's thought that only a couple of people have ever witnessed what goes on there. Every few years, there's a mysterious truck that shows up at the lighthouse. The legend goes on to say that in the dead of night, a secret truck is loaded up by fishing boats. The fishing boats are called the caravan of the Great Lakes. Kane, are you positive they didn't see you."

"Why?" I asked.

The old man responded, "Because if they had seen you, you most likely would have been captured and killed."

"My teacher said that there was a disappearance at the State Park last week," said Joe. "But it was thought to have been a drowning in the

Big Sable River, just downstream from the Hamlin Lake dam. Maybe the drowning was actually him being captured and killed by the caravan."

The old man said, "What if, and what if pigs could fly?. Don't waste your time messing around with this stuff. It's just an old wise tale. Some people believe in it and others think it's crazy."

"I know it's true!" I stated. "I saw the caravan and the truck with my own eyes. I just don't know what they are up to."

The old man mumbled in a mean tone "It's a long shot, go ahead and look into it for yourself. You're only wasting your time and energy."

Joe and I left with a great feeling, and a better idea about the mysterious activity that was going on at the Ludington State Park.

Chapter Three

The following day, Joe and I set out with a plan. We reserved the State Park campsite near the trail that led out to the lighthouse, which was the road the semi had taken from Big Point Sable, back into the State Park. We left early evening, around 6 PM to set up camp. I brought everything I thought would be helpful, including my Mini Moto dirt bike, with a sand tire, and a super quiet muffler so no one would hear me riding.

It was mid-summer and the sun was setting around 9:30, so we set up our fire and lathered up in bug spray.

Time dragged on and nothing was happening. Joe began complaining so I told him to go for a swim in Big Sable River to wake himself up. This was a big mistake, the river is known for an odd under current, where the river dumps into Lake Michigan. People can get pulled out into Lake Michigan and drown. It makes it even more dangerous at night when there's no one around watching to help a swimmer if they start to struggle.

After about a half-hour, I went to check on Joe, who had left to swim in the river. After five minutes of searching, I knew something was wrong. I couldn't find Joe, but I found his shirt and shoes. I started to freak out and started to yell for Joe. After about a half an hour of searching, I found footsteps on the opposite side of the river, but something was odd. The State Park has a beach tractor that cleans the litter of people every night near the shoreline. The beach had already been cleaned and all the footsteps from the day had been covered up. There were two sets of footprints on the freshly cleaned sand. At some point, it appeared that someone had been dragged through the sand. I went back to our campsite and threw all of our gear it into the bed of my old rusted out pickup truck.

I drove as fast as I could to Joe's house to tell his parents what had happened. They contacted the police and the next day, they sent out a search party for Joe. The search party started around seven in the morning; however, it was too late to find Joe. State Park visitors had already set up on the beach and there were footsteps going in all different directions.

Joe's parents were helping with the search, they both were in tears. I ensured them that I thought Joe was still alive and he would eventually turn up.

Later that week, I woke up in the morning to a strange knock on my front door. I went to open it, and it was a man from the FBI wanting to ask me questions about Joe. I let the man in and called my mom downstairs so she could be a part of the conversation. He told me how they found a body washed up onshore and it was the body of Joe. The FBI agent went by the name of Richard Monroe. I mumbled to myself, "Nice first name, what's Richard stand for?"

My mom heard me and kicked my shin from under the table because she didn't know what was going on. The agent explained to us what he thought had happened. Mom was scared for me to answer any questions, so she escorted the agent to the door. When he was leaving I told the agent something seemed off with his version of events and I was going to figure it out.

Chapter Four

Later I went back to the Old Hamlin, the only place I knew where I could get reliable information. I ordered some fries and a pop and waited and waited. It must have been my lucky day. The old man Joe that I had talked to previously walked into the restaurant. I ran over to him and said, "I need your help."

I told him the entire story of how my friend disappeared, and how there were footsteps on the other side of the river. I even told him about how the FBI found his body washed up on the shore.

In a panicked voice, the old man said, "I've never known the FBI to be involved in something like this. Did the agent give you his badge number?"

Flustered, I flipped through all the paperwork the agent had left me until I found the number. I gave it to the old man. He then asked my waitress if he could make a couple calls. He went back behind the counter. I could hear him on the phone, the concern in his voice was unmistakable. When he came back to my table, he had a worried look on his face. He said, "Son, the FBI doesn't have an agent by that badge number. There's some sort of imposter on the loose and the FBI told us to let them know if he comes by again. If he does, they want us to contact the police immediately."

I asked the old man if there was any more information he had about the caravan and the smuggling because I had a feeling this has something to do with it.

He said, "No, but there is one piece of information that could be useful. Yesterday, I was talking with one of my fellow breakfast companions and he told me this story about Peter Pan Land, a cliff that overlooks Lake Michigan. It is believed that back when only Indians lived in this area, a treasure map was placed within the side of a cliff. The only known cliffs still around to this day is Peter Pan Land. Go there and look for this map. Find it, and if it's true, it could lead you to your friend and maybe gold."

"Hold up, I'm confused," I stated. "How would something from ancient times be known of in modern times? "

The old man began, "It's to be believed that there have been several maps hidden all around the world. Find one, and claim the power of riches. My theory is that a group of thieves found one of these maps and located its treasure. They became greedy wanting even more money and power. So they started to steal gold from other countries. They thought Ludington would be the perfect place to hide it. I know it's a long shot but it's the only thing that adds up."

I shook his hand, "Thank you," I said, and ran to my house to grab my dirt bike.

I had an idea, but I needed help. I decided to ask Jordan, a good friend of mine. On the way to his house, a car blew a red light and smashed into a light pole. It was the craziest thing I had ever seen. I was in such a rush to Jordan's house; it never crossed my mind to stop and help the man. When I arrived at Jordan's, he had the radio on. The local radio station WKLA was reporting news about the accident. Police were saying that the man that was in the car accident had what appeared to be a fake FBI badge in the front seat.

This got me curious and I had to know more. I asked Jordan if he'd help me with this mystery. As soon as Jordan heard gold, he was all in. Our first task was to go to Peter Pan Land and find this ancient map.

On the way, we stopped by the hardware store on Ludington Avenue. I purchased as much rope as we could carry on my little dirt bike, which wasn't a lot, but hopefully it would do.

Chapter Five

We arrived at the two-tracks off Lakeshore Dive that leads into Peter Pan Land. I started to walk my dirt bike through the woods. I did not want to cause any sort of commotion, I figured it would be best to stay quiet.

I put my bike against a tree and we walked up to the sand cliffs edge. The cliffs at Peter Pan Land drop almost straight down for a few hundred feet to the edge of Lake Michigan. I took the rope and tied it around the tree. I asked Jordan if he wanted to go first, which of course he said no. I started to climb down the rope, but I was scared. The soft sandy ground was starting to give out from underneath me.

On the way down I saw bottle stuck in the side of the cliff. It had a doll head inside it, and the bottle read, "Stay out."

I reached out to grab the bottle, but as soon as I moved it, the ground started to shake. I started climbing down the cliff faster and faster, hoping that the rope wouldn't break. I was afraid I would fall and go crashing into Lake Michigan below. I finally made it down to a ledge on the cliff. There was a cutout in the wall. It read, "Only Those Known of GOD Can Enter".

I looked to my left and right, and that's when I saw it.

To my right, there was an entrance to the cave. I took a couple steps in. I yelled up to Jordan to come down. The entrance was dark and it appeared that there was an old carved wood door. Jordan said, "When you moved that doll head a ton of sand fell down the cliff's face into the lake below. I bet that sand was covering this entrance and this door."

We took out the flashlights we had brought, opened the door and started our way down the tunnel.

The end of the tunnel opened into a big room. In the middle of the room, there appeared to be a stand with some sort of paper on it. Jordan said, "Maybe that's the map we are looking for. But wait, look at the floor it looks booby-trapped."

The floor looked like a puzzle. Using my knowledge and some reasoning, we figured out the correct path we should take. Carefully one foot over the other, we made our way to the stand; however, at the stand, I found something shocking. The paper on the stand wasn't a map. It read FBI, with the agents' badge number on it. There was also a bunch of writing in different languages I couldn't read.

We left the cave immediately and headed to the police station. We asked if there could be any possibility to see the dead FBI agent's valuables. The detective investigating the accident said no, that it was impossible. We asked the detective if they found some sort of map on the man, and he told us only a road map.

It then crossed my mind and I asked the detective where the wrecked car was. He told me it had been towed to Marek's junkyard, just east of town. I thought to myself, "Great."

It was pretty easy to find the crashed car when we arrived. It was sitting right in front, the car said FBI right across the side. I walked up and opened up the passenger door. It was a miracle, the map we had been looking for was sitting right on the seat.

On the map, we found an "X," right on Ludington's harbor lighthouse. On the bottom of the map, it read "FOG," in small black letters. We decided it was getting late and we had to go home.

The following day was a big day. We knew we had to act fast. As more and more time went by, we knew there was less of a chance of finding Joe alive. We started by visiting the Ludington Lighthouse. The lighthouse is open for tours daily from 10AM – 2PM for $5 each. We joined the tour and climbed the stairway to the top. Jordan came up with a theory. He wondered if the clue we found had to do with the foghorn of the lighthouse. We made our way into the small room at the top of the lighthouse. The room had windows on every side, it's where the light and fog horn is operated. There it was! On the floor of the small room was a lock with a four letter combination. Each dial had every letter of the alphabet. I curiously ask the tour guide, "What is this combination dial?"

He responded and said, "No one knows. We are not allowed to have visitors guess the combination because the dials are getting stuck from the beach sand. Since you asked and the rest of your tour has already started down, give it a try I won't say anything."

The man said he would let us each try one word. All of a sudden, Jordan had one of the brightest moments in his life. He said, "What was inside that bottle that you lifted up on Peter Pan Land?"

After a few moments of thinking, I remembered and I tried my four-letter word. The room walls shifted slightly, revealing what appeared to be another clue. On the wall, it read, "To the smartest man of them all, only one can find the falls." The second message read, "To the man who has no power, only a three could be the key."

I wrote the two messages down so I wouldn't forget them. Now Jordan and I had another code to crack. My biggest question was where in the world would there be falls in Ludington? Jordan and I were hungry so we decided to go to the store and buy some junk food for lunch.

Chapter Six

    While at the store, a tourist was going through the Ludington postcards. She kept turning the rack that held the postcards, and that's when I saw it. There was a card that said Ludington State Park. On it, there was a picture of the state parks dam with water flowing down from it like a waterfall. I quickly grabbed the card and showed Jordan. I told him to leave his candy because we needed to go.

    We hopped on my dirt bike and sped down the road to the State Park. Entering into the park, we made a right and headed to the back. I looked at the messages again from the lighthouse and repeated to myself, " To the man who has no power, to the man who has no power, to the man who has no power."

Then, I got an idea that made my whole body shiver. I thought to myself, maybe the power is the falls crashing down and we need to stop them. I asked Jordan and he said, "Look, there are three wheels up at the top of the dam that appear to control the water level in Hamlin Lake. Let's go up there and see if we can stop the water from flowing over the falls.

At the top, I started to turn the first wheel to the left and more and more water rushed out of Hamlin Lake into Big Sable River. I then started to turn the wheel the other way, and the water slowly stopped. I looked down the cement where they water typically rushed. On the floodgate I closed, there was some sort of metal lever. I went first, and Jordan followed.

We slowly went across the cement and stone that the water usually crashed onto. It was slippery because of all the green algae and bacteria growing on it. All of a sudden, I heard a smack across the ground! Jordan had slipped on the cement and smacked his face. It looked like he broke his nose.

He rolled on the ground screaming in pain. I rushed over to him as quickly as I could. Once I calmed him down, he said he thinks he tore something in his leg. I told him he had to get up and keep going because time was precious. He soldiered on and I finally made it to the metal lever and pulled it up. I waited, and nothing happened. I kept reading in my head, "Only a three could be the key, only a three could be the key, only a three could be the key."

I decided to head back to the top of the dam and shut off all three of the dams watergates. Jordan stayed at the base of the dam. His leg started to swell up pretty bad and it was discolored with bruising.

Finally I got all the water to stop from flowing over the dam. Once I got down to the bottom, I looked at the wall and there were now 3 metal levers. I slowly walked across the stone and pulled the middle lever, but still nothing happened. I worked my way to the last lever and pulled it, hoping something would happen. I waited a couple of seconds, but still nothing.

Jordan yelled from across the river, "Maybe when it 'says 3 is the key,' it means you have to pull all 3 levers at the same time."

I yelled back, "Well how do you suppose I do that?"

Jordan cleverly replied, "Take the rope that we bought for Peter Pan Land and cut it into three smaller pieces. Tie each rope to a different lever and hold onto all three ropes at the exact same time and pull."

I thought to myself, "Since when had Jordan actually gotten smart."

I did everything Jordan told me to do, and I walked with the rope to the middle edge of the stone.

Jordan yelled, "On the count of three. One, two, three."

I yanked on all three ropes as hard as I could. Each lever rose up at the same time, and the dam and the ground started to shake. A pit opened up and I could see a stairwell leading down.

Chapter Seven

I walked over to the edge, where I saw spider webs covering the staircase. I told Jordan it was his turn to go first, even though he could barely walk. He obliged but said, "I call sixty percent of the riches if we find any."

I thought to myself, 60%, that's a horrible idea, but I gladly agreed so that I didn't have to go first. We slowly walked our way into the tunnel which appeared to be a maze. We finally came up to the first fork in the tunnel. We had to choose between five different directions. I told Jordan we should follow the far right one because it looked the most traveled; however, we soon realized that we made a huge mistake. All of a sudden we saw a light. This was no ordinary light; it was a flashlight with a blue bulb just like the headlights on the semi-truck.

We turned around and slowly started heading for the exit when a man saw us and yelled, "Hey, stop right there!"

We took off running and instead of leaving the tunnels, we took the middle one of the five tunnelways. As soon as we stepped through the doorway, the walls on both sides started to close, trapping us in. We could hear the man yell out to a couple of his buddies, "I think they went this way."

We heard their footsteps go down another tunnel, but we still had a huge problem. We were trapped inside the tunnel with only one way to go.

I asked Jordan softly, "What do we do now?"

"We follow this tunnel. It's the only thing we can do," Jordan replied.

We started to walk down the tunnel and I swear it was never going to end. Suddenly, we came to a hole that was filled with water.

"Should we jump in?" Jordan asked.

"I don't know, I bet its deeper than we think,"
I responded.

Jordan mumbled, "I'll go first, I don't really care. My leg is throbbing and maybe the cold water will numb the pain."

He jumped in and the water instantly went over his head. He took a deep breath and swam down under the water. I waited for what seemed like minutes and he never came up. I decided I should jump in because either he needs help or he came out on the other side. I jumped in and swam downwards about ten yards and continued at this depth for a few moments. Running low on air, I swam quicker and quicker through the water. Finally it felt like the tunnel started to go back upwards. I pushed off the bottom of the tunnel to help propel myself to the top. I then realized I had dropped my flashlight in the process. I tried to go back and grab it, and that's when everything went dark.

The next thing I remember was that I was laying on my back on hard cement with Jordan doing chest compressions on me.

I started to cough and then mumbled, "What happened?"

Jordan responded, "You almost drowned. I had to jump back into the hole to get you. I've been doing CPR for almost 2 minutes. I thought you were a goner."

I looked around and was curious about what we were sitting in. It was an extremely small room and Jordan had his flashlight lying on the ground facing up, the light beam reflecting off the ceiling. At the top, there was what appeared to be a hatch with a ladder leading to it. I sat up and started to cough up water. I then asked, "I wonder where that leads to?"

Jordan responded, "I think it could lead to the surface, but I'm not sure. It could be an escape route of some sorts. This tunnel hasn't led me to believe there are any riches at the end of it."

I told Jordan I'd climb up first because he went first the last time. As I climbed up the ladder, I felt weak.. I tried twisting the round hatch handle at the top, but it wouldn't budge. I grabbed Jordan's flashlight and started banging on the handle as it seemed to break free suddenly. I twisted it completely and pushed the hatch up. Blinded by the light from outside, I Squinted my eyes. I climbed out of the hole and Jordan quickly followed. When I got out, I realized we must've walked a lot farther than I thought because we were in the middle of the woods.

I took a look around, wondering if I could see anything I recognized. To my right appeared to be a pond, and to my left, there was some sort of hut. Jordan thought it was a bad idea to go into the hut, but I didn't listen. We walked over to the hut which looked a lot smaller from the distance. There was a sign on the door and it read, "Trespassers keep out."

"Kane, I don't think we should knock. This doesn't look safe," Jordan said.

I knocked anyway and the floor beneath us gave out as we started to fall. Time seemed to slow down and all of a sudden, we landed in a net.

Chapter Eight

All around us appeared to be dirt walls and that's when I noticed we weren't alone. There were maybe a total of fifty people working. I don't know exactly what they were doing, but it appeared to be some sort of mine. Workers were walking past and that's when I saw Joe. He was in the middle of the working crew and didn't seem to acknowledge that we were there.

Jordan and I climbed out of the net and hid behind a mining car. I yelled for Joe when he walked past and waved him over to us. He stepped aside and hid with us. He was shaking and said, "Get out, don't let them see you, they will kill you and eat you alive."

"Who will?" I squeaked back.

But it was too late, Joe ran back and got back to work immediately. Suddenly, all the workers got to their knees and faced the same wall, bowing down. A man walked through the doors. He wore a fur coat and what appeared to be a pair of slippers. He yelled out, "Workers, I have come to announce that any worker underperforming will be put to death. We need this gold and I don't want anyone to slow me down!"

I looked around to see if I could make sense of anything. I saw some workers leaving through a door, taking stuff in wheelbarrows. I figured that, that was where the gold was located as the door was opened by a worker. My mind raced to come up with a plan. It was kind of a long shot, so I asked Jordan, "What if we acted as workers, we could blend in and work our way to where that door is."

Jordan responded in a panicked voice, "Yes, it's about the only option I see that would work. We're trapped down here, and if we don't act fast, they are going to find us and we are going to die."

We jumped into the group of workers and grabbed a pickaxe and started to work. I slowly started to work my way over to the entrance. Once we got close enough, I dropped the pickaxe and walked through the door, acting as if I owned the place. I thought to myself, "If I acted more confident there would be less room for questions by the other workers."

My theory was correct however my theory about what was inside the room was incorrect. It was mine carts filled with gold ready to be pushed down the tracks. I said to Jordan, "Hurry and jump into that cart. Maybe if we're quick enough we can push ourselves down the track and go to wherever this takes us."

"Swell idea," Jordan replied.

We ran over to the mining car and started pushing. I pushed so hard my feet started to slip out from underneath me. We finally got it going and jumped in.

At first, I thought it was going to be an easy ride. All of a sudden, the cart started to pick up speed. Soon we were going at what I estimated to be around forty to fifty miles per hour. Weaving back and forth down the tracks, I thought we were going to fly over the edge. At one point I felt the right side's two wheels come off the tracks. I thought to myself, "How in the world is this cart going to come to a stop without smashing into something."

All of a sudden the cart started to go up and down long steep hills as it started to come to a stop. The cart made a left turn and that's when we saw it. It looked like and endless pile of gold.

I hopped out of the cart and started to walk around in amazement, quickly realizing that we were being watched. I saw it out of the corner of my eye, a man about 5 feet tall watching us. He was standing behind one of the tall pillars, that was holding up the huge room. I looked around trying to find some sort of exit. On the other side, there was a tall opening which appeared to be like an arc. I looked over at Jordan and pointed with a head nod. He winked at me and we started to run towards the opening.

As we were running I started to pick up gold, stuffing all I could into my pockets. We ran through the arc and it led us into another room that appeared to be part of a house. On the other side of the room there was a door, and then I heard a man yelling, "Get back here!"

We continued to the door and pushed it open. As we walked through, it slammed shut behind us. It led to the main portion of the house and there was a spiral staircase. All the windows were boarded up with cracks of lights coming through. I saw the front door and made my move for it. The door had about eight different locks on them. The first seven opened easily, but the last one gave me trouble. I couldn't get it open and I got flustered. I heard footsteps on the other side of the door we just came through and I started to shake with fear. I grabbed the first thing I saw, which was a medal vase, and slammed down on the lock. As the lock busted off, I heard the door behind us opening and I screamed, "RUUUUUN!!!!!!!"

Jordan and I bolted out the door and ran outside. We were in the middle of the woods, completely lost. I looked back and the house was right in front of a huge cliff. That explains how there was an entire tunnel system behind us and why no one has ever discovered this before. We kept running until I ran out of breath and then we walked the remainder. I kept looking over my shoulder to make sure we weren't being followed.

Chapter Nine

My first thought was for us to get out of the woods and back to Ludington as soon as possible. We needed to inform the police or something.

It felt like we were walking for miles on end. I had no idea how much progress we were making. I said to Jordan, "If we don't make it out of these woods by nightfall, we could end up dying out here, a lot could go wrong."

Of course, the sun started to set and we weren't out of the woods. We were in for an interesting night.

"Hey Jordan, we should take cover by those big trees over there," I said.

Jordan responded, "Yeah, we could find some fallen branches and set them up against the trees to sleep under."

I proceeded to look for large fallen branches. Luckily Jordan had an extra flashlight because I lost mine when I almost drowned back inside the tunnels. I was having trouble but then I found the jackpot. There appeared to be a tree that had fallen a long time ago. Most of the tree had been dried out so it was easy to snap the branches off. I called Jordan over and asked him for his help to help me carry the branches. We carried them back to the large tree and set them up to make a small little fort to keep ourselves less visible and out of harm's way. That's when I heard a weird sound coming from the distance.

The sound almost appeared to be like an animal whimpering or crying. I decided to investigate and left our little hut. I climbed over a couple of newly fallen trees. The sound was coming closer so I knew I was going in the right direction. The sound suddenly sounded as if it was right on top of me, mocking me as if it knew I was looking for it. All of a sudden my flashlight beam struck an object that looked like a tail.

I walked over to it and found a cute little dog rolled up into a ball, as if it hadn't eaten in days. I gently said, "Are you lost little guy? Here, come with me."

I picked him up and carried him back to the fort. I reached into my pocket and pulled out a piece of beef jerky so that he could eat. He scarfed the food down with no problem. I decided to sacrifice the last of my water for the dog because he looked like he could use it more than me.

I ended up falling asleep with my head laying on my bag and the dog laid his head right across my chest. I woke up in the morning and couldn't tell what part of the day it was because I couldn't see the sun through the woods. Jordan was still asleep and so was the dog. I decided to wake up Jordan so we could start our long walk out of these woods. Jordan woke up and the dog woke up as well. Jordan said, "Why is there a dog here."

"I found him last night and he was whimpering, so I decided to take him with us," I responded.

Jordan said rudely, "How could we trust this wild dog? He could have rabies or something."

We started to walk and we didn't make it far before the dog started to take his own way. I told Jordan we should follow the dog because he might know the way out. As we were walking, I noticed something strange. There were a lot of different mounds throughout the woods that didn't make any sense to me. Finally, after walking for several hours we made it to a fence in the woods. It had barbed wire at the top, and a sign which read, "Indian burial ground. No TRESPASSING!!!!!"

I told Jordan, "Well that explains why there were all those mounds while we were walking through the woods."

We found a part in the fence where the barbed wire was cut off. I climbed it and once I reached the top, I told Jordan to hand the dog to me. As I jumped off the top of the chain link fence my leg got caught and made a deep scratch on the skin on my calf. Jordan then jumped the fence. The dog started to lick all the blood off my leg. I pushed him away and I said to Jordan, "What should we name the dog?"

"I think we should name him Dylan, like my crazy friend," Jordan responded.

With the dogs name settled, we continued with our walk. After about an hour we made it out of the woods. I didn't know exactly where we were but we saw a couple of houses and Jordan happily yelled, "I know where we are. We are on the opposite side of Hamlin Lake.

We decided to walk up to one of the houses and ask for a ride back into town. The first house we knocked at was blue, but no one answered. The next house was a yellow house and an older gentleman answered. I said, "Hi, my name is Kane and this is

Jordan. We've been lost in the woods and need a ride back into town."

Chapter Ten

The man agreed and took us into town, dropping us off at the police station. Before we got out of the car I asked the man for his name and he said, "Scottie."

I walked in and asked for the sheriff. It took about a half an hour but he finally showed up and said, "What can I help you with?"

I responded, "This is my friend Jordan and my name is, Kane. I would like to inform you about something that's going on in Ludington State Park. My friend and I just came out of the Indian Burial ground and I think there are some thieves under the Hamlin Lake Dam stealing and hiding gold."

The officer cut me off short, "How do you know about our secret criminal organization?"

Within about two seconds officers were surrounding us. One grabbed my arms and cuffed me behind the back. Another officer came over and put a bag over my head. I was dragged to one room and I could hear Jordan yelling and screaming in another. The screaming eventually stopped. Fifteen minutes later the door opened up, I heard footsteps and the door closed again. Someone sat down in a chair and in a deep, nasally voice someone screamed, "Tell me what you know!"

I knew we were in for a long ride once I heard the man's voice. I just got to thinking to myself, what in the world is going on here. The cops are in on this too? I started thinking harder and thought to myself, I wonder if these criminals are paying the police department in gold to keep their mouths shut.

The idea was genius, but at the same time could cause this entire city to go under. All of a sudden I heard a loud, "Bang!"

It almost sounded like a gunshot. The officer in front of me said, "What it the world was that?"

As the sound of the next bang went off I heard Dylan barking. Thank God he was still alive I thought to myself. The officer that had started to question me had now left the room. As soon as I heard the door slam, the sound of what was definitely an automatic rifle started going off. The door opened and a woman's voice rang out, "Are you okay? I'm with YYCP and I'm here to save you from these criminals. Are they holding anyone else besides you?."

"Yes," I frantically responded. "My friend was taken to another room I believe."

The lady ran over to me, removed my handcuffs and took the bag off my head. I stood up and looked at the lady. She was a tall lady about 6 foot 1. She wore black pants with a blue sweatshirt and a bulletproof vest overtop. She ran to the other room and grabbed Jordan. As she was walking back to me she noticed the large cut on my leg. "What happened to your leg?" she asked.

I quickly responded, "I don't want to talk about it."

She ran over to the front of the police station and grabbed her bag. She pulled out a first aid kit and from it, she pulled out what appeared to be alcohol and stitches. She looked at my cut and determined it was too deep to heal without stitches. "Close your eyes this is going to sting," she said.

She started to pour the alcohol and I started to scream in pain. I yelled, "Stop, stop, stop!"

As she kept pouring the alcohol she finally stopped and started to dab the wound with a cloth. She then picked up the stitching and started to stick the needle through my wound to sew it up. I don't remember much of it because I passed out from the pain.

When I woke up, I was being driven in a car by a lady I did not recognize. We were driving on the US 31. Dylan and Jordan were also in the car with me. I said in a panicked tone to Jordan, "What are we doing? How did we get into this car? And who's driving?"

"She's part of the YYCP, one of the largest and well-known spy agencies know," Jordan responded.

The lady chimed in, "I'm agent 504 also known as Nova."

"Ok, where are we going?" I asked.

Nova responded, "There's a yellow house out at the beginning of the countryside. I know the owners and they're letting my crew set up there. We have about twenty-five agents located at the house. We've been tracking the criminals that you guys just got mixed up with."

"How dangerous are these guys?" I asked.

All of a sudden Dylan started barking out the back window. I looked back and Nova yelled, "Crap, I think they're onto us!"

Jordan frantically said, "Who's onto us?"

"They call themselves the Wanderers. They know we're onto them. We can't let them find our base," Nova stated.

I responded quickly, "Take them down the side roads and try to lose them."

Nova started to floor it, and the car took off faster than a dog running for a rabbit. I looked at the back of the seat and it said Corvette. That explains why the car accelerates faster than any other car I've ever been in.

We started turning on back roads. At one point we reached over one-hundred miles per hour. Confident that we had finally lost them, we started to head back to the base. Nova hit the garage button and we pulled in, but it was no ordinary garage. It went down underground and opened up into a large parking garage. There were all sorts of military vehicles and sports cars.

At the back of the garage, there was an opening that looked like a spy base with a bunch of different people working. We got out of the car and made our way over to a man who was waiting for us.

The man said, "Ohhh, Nova I see you brought people in off the streets again. How did you get these suckers?"

She responded, "Well I rescued them from the police station. The police are in on this too, and they had these kids hostage."

"What's your name son?" the man asked me.

Jordan cut me off, "I'm Jordan and this is my friend Kane. We've been away from home for a while and our parents are probably worried sick."

"Don't worry, we'll be contacting your parents very soon. Our best spy has already got your parents names and he will be contacting them about your situation," he reassured us.

We walked over to a computer and he went over everything that was happening in Ludington. He talked about the trucks with the blue headlights and how the SS Spartan is bringing stolen gold from Canada, and they are hiding all of it underneath the Ludington State Park. The agent's mission is to somehow stop them, but because they are heavily armed, it's not going to be that simple.

I then proceeded next by asking the man what his name was. He said he goes by Agent 503 and nothing else.

Agent 503 then asked, "So who's this little guy?"

"Oh, that's Dylan. Kane found him the night we were trapped in the Indian burial ground," Jordan responded.

The man lit up. "You were in the burial ground. How in the world did you get all the way out there?" he asked.

I chimed in, "Well, you know that dam in the state park. We discovered there is a tunnel system under the dam. We discovered that's where they have been keeping their gold."

"You what? How in the world did you get in there? That park is crawling with security to make sure no one even comes close to discovering anything about those tunnels," said Agent 503.

Time started to go by fast and before I knew it the big clock on the top of the spy base read 9:54.

Agent 503 decided it was time for bed so he escorted, Jordan, Dylan, and I to a room in the back. It was a comfy room with all sorts of fans blowing around the room. I fell asleep with Dylan laying his head on my shoulder and the next thing I knew, it was 7 o'clock and a trumpet started to go off. I thought to myself, "Really? Why in the world do they need to get up so early and why use a trumpet?"

I got up and agent 504 walked in front of the door. She pointed over to a door and said, "There's the bathroom and shower. In the bathroom there is also a closet with all new clothes for you to try on and wear.

I took a shower and Jordan followed suit after. We even gave Dylan a bath. He seemed to love the water, so he must be some sort of water dog.

I went over to the closet and they had all sorts of different clothes. They even had clothes for Dylan. I put on an all-black outfit and felt ready to go.

Jordan and I walked out into the main area and saw Agent 503 from across the room.

"Goodmorning," he yelled to us.

We made our way over to him and he started to ask us if we were ready to go on the mission. Jordan and I looked at each other. "What mission?" I nervously ask.

Agent 503 responded, "You guys are going to help our agents get into those tunnels under the dam. Our men have been looking for the entrance of that place for months."

He told Jordan and I that we were going with his best agents to ensure our safety. Agent 503 then called the agents over and I said, "What's up to all of them."

Oddly none of them responded or introduced themselves.

Chapter Eleven

We hopped into an SUV that, according to one of the agents, had bulletproof glass to ensure that we would feel safe. We took the highway all the way back into the city of Ludington and from there, we drove out to the State Park.

When we rolled up to the front entrance of the park, we were stopped by a park ranger, ensuring we had the appropriate park sticker on our license plate. As we drove away I noticed him call and talk on his radio, and then a car started to follow us.

The agent driving turned right as soon as we pulled in. We started driving towards the dam and more and more people started watching us. We pulled into a parking spot near the campground and got out of the car. All the agents were wearing beach clothes so they could blend in with the tourists. I knew people were watching us, but I didn't know who.

One of the agents hooked us up with walkie-talkies so we could all stay in touch in case we got separated.

As soon as we walked over to the dam, one of the agents asked where the entrance was. I tried explaining to him it wasn't that simple and I pulled them all aside for a game plan.

I told them that we needed three on the bottom of the dam and five on the top. The people on the top have to twist the wheels so that it stops the water from pouring down the dam. Once all the water stops there will be three different levers on the wall. At the same time, all three levers need to be pulled at the same exact time to open up the entrance.

We soon started to go through with the plan, and then things started to go south. We started to get shot at from the direction of the park entrance.

We retreat farther back into the park woods to shield ourselves from the bullets.

One of the agents radioed in for the boats on Hamlin Lake to come. Then in the next few seconds, he got shot in the arm. He stopped for a minute, but I think he realized he better pick up the pace or else he was going to die. We ran a few hundred yards upstream from the dam and there I saw a large pontoon boat waiting for us. We all jumped on and the boat sped off. It had two four-hundred horsepower engines and we were flying. I laughed as we passed the State Park swimming beach with the No Wake Zone sign.

A medic was on the boat and she was checking on the agent who had been shot in the arm.

The boat shot straight across the lake where we were transferred to a second boat that had dirt bikes and quads on it.

Agent 503 was on it and he said, "New game plan. All you guys are going to flank the dam. We are going to drop you off at the dunes over there and you're going to ride from the dunes to the shore of

Lake Michigan. You're then going to drive up to the Big Point Sable Lighthouse and take Lighthouse Trail into the State Park and then to the dam. Then you're going to get into the tunnel system, take it over, and give the gold to the FBI.

It was one of the finest dirt bike rides of my life. I started to jump the dunes as we made our way to the shoreline of Lake Michigan It was about a twenty-minute drive but felt good with the breeze in our faces. The only problem was the sun was blazing on my skin and I could feel it burning my skin like a slow roasting marshmallow.

Once we finally made it to the shoreline we started to cut up towards the lighthouse. That was another twenty-minute ride. I saw the peak of the lighthouse and saw no one was working at the top, which was perfect. We drove past the lighthouse and started to head down the trail.

Our bikes were making a lot of noise so we had to ditch them so we didn't tip off the criminals that we were coming. We walked about a mile to the back of the campground and we set up with the plan again.

Four agents walked up to the dam and over the top, acting as if they were normal people on a hike through the woods. They made their move and started to quickly shut the water of the dam off. Jordan, another agent, and I ran up to the bottom of the dam to pull the handles.

The agent started to run across the slippery cement and fell. He fell to the ground and slammed his head across the cement. I thought to myself, I know that hurts. He got back up and ran to the lever. I yelled "one, two, three" and we all pulled the levers at the same time.

The entrance of the tunnels opened and all the agents piled in; however, this time was different. The entrance shut immediately behind us and it appeared we were trapped inside.

The agents asked us which direction and Jordan told them to go through the right tunnel. This time each of the agents had a pistol with a flashlight. We started to make our way down the tunnel. "This is where we saw the flashlight coming last time," I said.

This time we made it past the point Jordan and I were at last time. It was a long walk and we finally made it to a room. This room, however, had a bunch of technology in it. It had a lot of television screens which were all turned off. One of the agents walked over to a screen and searched for the power button. Once he found it he clicked it on. It took a couple of seconds to boot up but soon the blue light hit my eyes. One of the agents said, "I've never seen any technology like this in my life. Look that appears to be a live recording of what's going on all around us. I think these criminals are pretty advanced for their time."

Everyone started to turn on the screens and we soon found out that we could everything that was happening in these tunnels.

One of the screens showed a crew of people working and they appeared to be moving boxes out of the tunnels. It seemed weird, and then on another screen, we saw workers, if you could even call them that. They were loading gold into the boxes. One of the agents said nervously, "They're moving the gold, they must be transporting it to another location."

We needed to act fast and try to get to that room so we can stop them.

One of the agents said, "Kane do you know how to get to where they are?"

I responded nervously, "Yes, but it's not safe, I almost drowned."

All the agents started to talk again and they came up with a new plan. They decided to go through the backdoor of the room we were in because they didn't want to risk anyone dying in these tunnels.

We started walking through the backdoor and all the agents had their guns drawn as we were walking because they didn't want to take any chances.

The farther we got into the tunnels the colder it got. I swear we walked at least a mile before we came to the large room where all the gold was, but by the time we made it, it was already too late.

One of the agents started to swear and was yelling some pretty profane things. They had been in search of this stolen gold for a long time and now they might have to start the search over.

We made our way out of the cave through the same hatch Jordan and I escaped from the last time.

This time we didn't have to walk through the woods to leave. All we had to do was find a big enough opening in the tree line and a helicopter came and picked us up.

It was about ten minutes until our rescue came and we flew back to headquarters. Agent 503 asked, "What happened, you guys were so close."

I answered, "They knew we were onto them and they didn't want to waste any time. They moved their gold out and they're moving it to another location as we speak."

"This is just great!" Agent 503 yelled.

He told us to go home and that we weren't needed anymore. On the way home, Jordan and I got really frustrated. We thought we had come across the greatest criminal bust of all time and we blew our opportunity. We could have been American heroes and saved the stolen gold.

A lot of time had passed and Jordan and I went on with our lives. About ten months had passed and we never heard again from Agent 503 or Nova.

Then one day my mom called me downstairs and said a girl by the name of Nova wanted to talk to me.

I picked up the phone and said, "Hello."

Nova said, "Kane, I was wondering if you wanted to help out the agents again?"

I said, "Yes, of course!"

She quickly responded and said, "Come outside in ten minutes, I'll be waiting for you."

I waited a few minutes and told my mom I had to leave. I ran outside to see where she was. She waved to me from her old beat-up car and I ran over to get in.

I got into the car and she said, "Games back on. We found the criminals again and where they're operating at. The passenger ship they were using is now used by the railroad to transport train cars, it's also open to the public. We believe they try to blend in with the passengers on board to help them stay undercover. The people on board cause a distraction so no one knows what they are doing. Now we believe they are getting stolen gold shipped to Wisconsin and from there, they load up train cars onto the Spartan and bring it over to Ludington. Once they bring it into harbor, they take it on semis and ship it out into the countryside onto a large farm."

I cut her off and said, "How far away is the farm?"

Nova answered and said, "It's just down the road from our yellow house. It was really pure luck that we found it. We had just about given up, when one morning one of our agents was on a run and he stumbled across this barn that look suspicious. The only problem is that it's one of the most heavily armed places we've ever had to deal with."

We drove back to the yellow base and on the way, I saw a lot of smoke over the tops of the trees. I didn't really think much about what it could've been, but when we made a left onto Chauvez Road where the spy base was on, I realized what it was. The smoke was coming from the yellow house. Nova started to scream, "Nooooo, they burnt it to the ground!"

Chapter Twelve

We drove up to the house that was burning, but I don't think it was as bad as Nova thought. The garage wasn't attached to the house and that's where the spy base was at, so I think everything is going to end up being okay.

We drove into the garage and ran into the base where we met Agent 503. He said, "Are you guys wondering why the house is on fire? We decided we didn't want to draw any attention to ourselves so we decided to burn the house to the ground."

I said, "Wouldn't the house burning down draw more attention to us?"

"Well, our theory is that if the criminals saw a building burning down, then they won't think it's us. I think they are starting to get a general sense of where we are located and we can't afford for that to happen," Agent 503 said.

We all headed outside and watched the firefighters outside put out the fire. They asked us what caused this fire and we all claimed we didn't know.

When the firefighters left, all that was left was a pile of black ashes and the toilet.

Agent 503 said, "Well the house we ordered will be here tomorrow."

"What house?" Nova asked.

Agent 503 responded, "Oh yeah we bought a double-wide house to cover up this mess. It will look great."

When we went back inside, Agent 503 informed us of all the new information they had concerning these criminals. They figured out the name of the organization leader. He goes by Ma Parker. He is one of the toughest criminals known to law enforcement and our mission is to capture him. If he's captured it will ruin all his plans due to the fact he is the only one who gives orders, and no one else is in line after him.

I asked Agent 503, "So, we are basically bounty hunters looking for this guy? How are we going to catch him? He has to have a lot of defenses and power. You saw what happened to us when we tried to enter into their tunnel system under the dam, now that is abandoned."

Agent 503 responded, "We believe Ma Parker has been living among us for as long as we have been here. He goes on with his everyday life just like the rest of the residents in Ludington. Our mission is to figure out who he is and capture him."

Everyone's mission for the day was to locate Ma Parker. Nova and I drove around for a long time and found nothing. I asked about the area that was on the other side of the harbor and if there was a possibility that they could be there.

Recently, I heard one person had rented out five of the condos at Crosswinds, over on the other side of the harbor. I thought that it was odd for someone to need five homes for themselves. Rumors spread quickly in a small town. A man named JD Garden had mentioned it to me.

I told Nova about the rumor I heard and she radioed the information to Agent 503. We decided to do a quick drive-by. She told 503 everything and that if we didn't contact him within a half-hour, to send help to our location.

Chapter Thirteen

We drove down Lakeshore Drive and rolled up to the entrance of the condominiums at the end of the road. As we approached the private entrance, we saw a lady in the window of the guard shack. We drove up and rolled our window down. Nova looked in and screamed. There was a manikin sitting in a chair trying to fool people into thinking there was a real guard.

I laughed and said, "Seriously, that dumb thing scared you. Aren't you supposed to be one of the top-ranked secret agents?"

"Shut up," Nova said jokingly.

We drove into the condos and parked the car along the curb. I got out and Nova asked, "What are you doing? We need to scout the area out before we get out of the car," Nova stated.

We sat in the car for who knows how long just watching everything to get an idea of the area. Nova radioed back to the base just so she could say the half-hour starts now. Within a few seconds, we had one of our largest discoveries thus far. Nova was playing with our radio and stumbled across a channel that had some sort of interesting code being broadcasted. The code was being repeated over and over and we had no idea what it meant. It didn't sound like a foreign language, but it didn't seem like random noises either.

We left immediately from the condos and headed back to base before investigating any more. The new house arrived a day early apparently because it was sitting on top of the old ash covered foundation. We entered the garage. Nova must've been in some sort of major rush because she smashed off one of the cars mirrors pulling into the garage.

She got out of the car and didn't turn it off. I was hoping that the ventilation system worked well because I wasn't trying to die from carbon monoxide poisoning.

She ran over and grabbed the agent specialized in cracking codes. He walked over and started to listen. He took out his pen and paper and started to write down what appeared to be a bunch of formulas. Minutes passed, eventually the minutes turned into hours.

Just when I thought there was no hope of cracking it, the agent came out of the car and said, "I've got it."

Nova screamed with joy. "You got it?" she asked."

The agent responded, "Yea I got the gum off the bottom of the seat that someone stuck there as he glanced at me."

"Wait you haven't gotten the code yet?" Nova asked.

"Oh, yea I got that an hour ago he said. It was really easy," the agent responded.

"What is it?" I asked.

The agent answered slowly, "It says, on the northernmost part of the five you will see me. Don't run, just ask to be."

I wondered what that meant, and then I had a good idea. I said, "Maybe it means that the guy that runs this entire operation stays in the fifth condo farthest north."

Everyone thought it was worth a shot and only Nova and I were sent out to see if we could confront this Ma Parker guy.

We arrived back at the condos and drove to the northernmost condo and knocked on the door. No one answered, so we walked around to the backdoor and looked in through the sliding glass door. That's when we saw him. A man was sitting in a chair not moving. His eyes were open and he showed no response. I banged harder and the man moved. He must've been sleeping with his eyes open.

He got up and walked to the door to slide it open. I said, "Hello Ma Parker."

His eyes lit up and he said, "How do you know me by that name?"

He reached into the back of his pant loop and pulled a gun quicker than I could even see. I heard the bang of a gun and looked down at my stomach. There was nothing wrong with me. I glanced to Nova as she was collapsing to the ground. Ma Parker took off while I radioed for assistance from the base.

Chapter Fourteen

Medics arrived and took Nova away as I fell to the floor in tears. Agent 503 picked me up as I was sitting on the curb thinking about everything that happened.

We drove to the Ludington hospital where Nova was being treated. On the way, Agent 503 was radioed with an update. Nova was going into emergency surgery and as of right now, they don't know if she was going to make it.

We arrived at the hospital and I ran in, asking where Nova was at. When Agent 503 and I arrived, Nova was still in surgery. The surgery lasted a little longer than four hours, The surgeon finally came out and told us the news. He said, "Hello everyone, you guys must be Nova's friends and family. I have some good news and I have better news.

Nova's surgery was very successful, In addition Nova has elected to participate in a medical treatment trial. We are now testing on humans a new technology accelerates the body's natural healing process and shortens recovery to seventy-two hours, Nova's wound qualified for this trial treatment.

"Can we see her now?" I asked.

The surgeon responded, "No you can't. She is still in recovery. You can visit her tomorrow at around noon."

We all left with a sense of anxiety. We were all wondering if she's actually going to be okay. I had faith in the doctor so I didn't feel like I had too much to worry about.

The next day arrived and all the agents had a team breakfast in the morning before we went to visit Nova. We had pancakes and bacon. I love bacon and I almost ate two pounds.

On the way to the hospital, I noticed something strange. There were a number of police cars out on patrol. Knowing that all the police were being paid off by the criminals, I was curious what was up. There's no one I could even tell about the police, I had no way to prove they're being paid off.

I didn't really think much of it, but when I entered the hospital, I asked the lady at the receptionist desk what room Nova was in. She said room 305 and when I walked into the room I couldn't believe what I saw.

A police officer was asking Nova questions and he said to Nova, "Thank you for your time, that's all I need."

He walked out of the room and looked me dead in the eyes before exiting. I said, "Nova, don't you remember the police are paid off by the criminals."

Her mouth dropped as she just realized she has just revealed to the criminals everything that happened to her.

The doctor said the treatment was going even better than anticipated and that Nova was good to be released from the hospital as soon as she signed some discharge documents.

We left the hospital and drove back to base to inform Agent 503 what Nova has done so we can limit the damage.

We arrived at the base and I left Nova in the car as I went to talk to Agent 503. I told him everything that happened and what I knew about Nova talking to the police. Agent 503 was outraged.

He left the room and slammed the door behind him. I heard him yelling in rage from behind the door. He kept swearing and I lost track of time, so I went back and got Nova. Nova was crying, realizing she might have ruined our chances of catching the criminals.

Chapter Fifteen

The next day, we set out in full force in search of the stolen gold. This time we weren't messing around. There were about eight cars and everyone was equipped in military attire.

All the agents had AK-47s besides me because I hadn't been properly trained to use one. All they gave me was some pepper spray and a taser that was disguised as a pen. If I was in any hand to hand combat, my chances of winning a fight would be slim to none. I could only hope that if someone shot at me, that they were the worst shot in the world.

We returned to condos at the end of Lakeshore Drive. Agent 503 had called the owner, confirming which five were rented by Ma Parker.

We sent most of the troops into the condo where Nova was shot. I walked into all five condos and looked around. Each room had one painting hanging on the wall. No one could tell what any of the paintings were. I looked at all five paintings and couldn't figure out what they were. I radioed to everyone in each condo. By this point I was in the condo that Nova was shot in. I said, "Can someone from each condo bring all the paintings into the condo Nova was shot at."

Soon agents started to bring the paintings to me and I laid them on the ground in the center of the room. I started to move them around and I saw a pattern within the paintings. I lined them all up in a specific order and the paintings made one large image.

Once the images were lined up we made a shocking discovery. It was a painting of a farm. I asked Nova, "Do you think that's the farm our agent found?"

She responded, "Yes, but it's not gonna be easy to get into. There aren't too many places guarded as closely as that farm is."

I told her confidently, "Well we do have a lot of agents and eight cars. It shouldn't take any more than a day to get into the farm.

The sun was setting and the moon was already in the sky. It was a full moon tonight, and there was an orange vibe to it. I had a feeling something was spooky about the night. Later in the night, around midnight, Nova and I decided to go on a walk outside. We walked through the cornfield behind the house and walked up to the front line of the woods.

I asked Nova, "Do you want to go into the woods?"

"Yeah sure," she said, "What is the worst that could happen?"

We entered into the woods and walked for a bit. I was moving my flashlight from side to side, ensuring that I didn't trip on any fallen trees or sticks. All of a sudden, my flashlight struck a red object. It looked like a truck that had been broken down for many years. We walked up to it and started to check it out. I popped open the glove box and there was still paperwork, and on the proof of insurance, it had JD Garden's name.

I showed it to Nova and she flipped out. She said, "I wonder if this trail leads to the farm we're breaking into."

We started walking down the trail and Nova followed closely behind. We were walking in the opposite direction from where our base was located. I didn't think it was a good idea to keep walking, but I didn't care. I was interested in what was at the end of the trail. The trail started to turn around a bend and I saw a light.

We moved up a little closer and noticed it was a light on the top of some sort of building. The closer we got, the more and more lights that appeared. Soon, we came up to a fence and the gate was open. I didn't mind myself and walked past the fence. All of a sudden, a motion sensor light kicked on. Nova and I jumped off the trail and into the woods.

Moments later, a man came from the building and started to look around the trail. He didn't look for long. A deer ran past and he must've just thought it was the deer. "Thank God," I thought to myself, "It doesn't get any luckier than that."

We started to advance up along the trail but we stayed in the woods so that we stayed out of the view of anyone. We made it up to the edge of the woods where the property began. We started to glance around as we could see just about everything. There were all sorts of lights on what appeared to be a barn. Nova whispered to me, "Do you think this is the farm we are looking for?"

I answered by saying, "I don't know, it very well could be. We need to stay low so we are not seen. If it is the farm, how was there no security over here?"

All of a sudden three large semis with blue headlights rolled onto the property and they flashed right at us, then turned away. I looked at Nova who looked back at me. Her eyes lit up and I knew she knew what this meant. We took off in the other direction for our base. We were running as fast as we could down the trail and all of a sudden, a set of headlights appeared behind us.

I looked back and started to run faster and faster, knowing we were almost back to the truck. I jumped into the woods and messed up my knee. Nova jumped right on top of me and we got as low as possible as the car drove by. I don't think the driver or anyone in the car saw us as it passed. All of a sudden the car went into reverse and stopped right in front of us. The window rolled down and I saw bright red eyes looking straight at us. Neither Nova nor I moved a muscle as the eyes didn't move off of us.

Chapter Sixteen

It was so quiet I could hear a pin drop on the ground and that's when I heard the seat belt unbuckle and the door unlock. Nova and I jumped up and started to run through the woods. I was falling behind as my knee started to sting and all of a sudden I fell to the ground. Nova continued to run not realizing what had happened to me. I turned back the other way to see if they were following us and that's when I knew I was in trouble.

I saw the red eyes moving swiftly through the woods, they were coming straight for me. The figure grabbed me by the arm and someone threw a cloth bag over my head. It began dragging me through the woods back to the car. I heard the trunk pop and then I was thrown in. The trunk slammed and I started to scream. I knew I was in for major trouble.

I took the bag off my head and the car started to speed down the trail. The driver suddenly slammed on the breaks and it felt like he turned the wheel as sharp as he could. The tail of the car whipped around. I think we did a one-eighty and we started to travel in the other direction back towards the barn.

I couldn't tell for sure how fast we were traveling but I'd say around fifty miles per hour. One wrong maneuver and we'd be smashed into a tree.

I thought to myself, at our speed we should be back to the barn soon. Who knew what they were going to do with me. All of a sudden, the driver slammed on the breaks again. I heard a garage door open and I grabbed the radio I forgot I had in my pocket. I tried radioing to Nova, but for some reason it didn't work. I wondered if my signal was being blocked.

I started thinking of all the horrible things they might do to me trying to get me to talk.

The car started to move again and stopped again about 20 feet later. I heard the garage door start to shut and once it closed completely, the trunk of the car popped open. A man lifted it the rest of the way and said, "Get out."

He had two other friends with him. They dragged me away into another room where they searched me. They put everything I had in my pockets on the table.

I asked the man, "Who are you?"

He shot back, "I was just about to ask you that." He continued, "Well if you would really like to know, my name is Ma Parker and I am a well-known criminal. You can find me on America's most-wanted list. The only thing that separates me from any other criminals is that I can bribe my way out of anything."

"You better hope so. I'm working with a team of special agents, they are after you right now," I said.

He creepily responded, "That was easy... I didn't even need to ask you anything, you just gave me everything I needed to know."

He started to yell orders in a foreign language and I couldn't tell what he was saying. A couple of guys nodded their heads and walked away.

I thought to myself again, what in the world is this guy gonna do to me? I then said something that I would soon regret for the rest of my life. I looked at the man and said, "So your JD Gardens?"

His head snapped back at me. "What did you just say?" He asked.

He jumped up and grabbed a baseball bat and started to smash everything. "How do you know that name?" he yelled.

I scrambled for an answer, "Um, um, the agents. They gave me all the information about you and your criminal organization. They talked about how you paid off all the police here so they would keep their mouths shut," I said.

He left the room when I prepared for when he got back. I got up and grabbed the pen I had because I knew it could come in handy at some point.

He came back and threw a pillow at me. That's when I knew I'd be spending the night in this creepy barn. I slept on some dirt and folded my pillow up to elevate my head.

I woke to the sound of the garage door opening and a man shaking me. He told me to get into the car. I got up, walked to the car and we sped away down the trail.

For a minute I thought I was being rescued but I soon realized that it was Ma Parker tearing off down the trail with me in the passenger seat. I asked him what was going on and he told me that the barn we thought the gold was at was just a staging area, and the gold's hidden back in Peter Pan Land.

I knew it. I thought it was strange that we found the gold that easy after it was in one of the best hiding spots known to man. Ma Parker said, "Yeah, do you remember that cave at Peter Pan Land? If you jumped into the water and swam down about five feet and then swam about ten feet back towards the cliff, and back up, you would find the cave with all of the gold. Little did you know you were right on top of it the entire time."

I asked him where we were going and he responded saying, "To the cave where the gold is."

"Why are we going there?" I asked.

"Because it's the only place your dang agents don't know about," he responded.

We drove and turned left onto Iris Road right before the Pere Marquette River and started to make our way towards Lake Michigan. When the road ended we made a left onto Lakeshore Drive. We continued till we came to the dirt half-loop off the side of the road. We ditched the car and started to walk up the sandy trail. A huge cliff was to the right, and a sand dune to the left. He grabbed my wrist as we walked down the sand dune to the water's edge.

He said, "Jump in and swim down about five feet down. Then swim back into the cliff and up."

I did exactly what he said and I popped out in the cave where I saw endless amounts of gold. Soon Ma Parker came up through the water and he pointed me over to an area that appeared to be a living area with a couch. I walked over and sat down.

Ma Parker sat in front of me on another chair and that's when I started to smirk. I looked him dead in the eyes and couldn't help myself as I started to laugh.

"Why are you laughing?" Ma Parker said with a concerned look.

"You didn't know," I responded. "I've been chipped by the agents. There's a tracking device that has been put inside my arm so they know exactly where I am right now."

Chapter Seventeen

Ma Parker jumped up in urgency. He ran over
to his radio and I could hear him requesting backup.
Before I knew it, there were about thirty of his
criminals in the tunnels with fully automatic weapons
watching the entrance.

The night rolled around and still no sign of any
of our agents. I was thinking to myself that they
must have been searching the barn for the gold.

I fell asleep on the couch and woke up to the
sound of a gunshot. I looked up in hopes that the
agents had made their way to save me, but one of Ma
Parker's workers fell to the ground as Ma Parker was
holding a gun to the back of his his workers head. I
got back down, afraid to make any sort of movement
to tip-off that I was watching him.

Once morning came around, I had a throbbing headache. I haven't drank any water in over nineteen hours and I think I was finally feeling dehydrated. I asked Ma Parker for some water and then he spit on me for giving up the location of his base.

All of a sudden I noticed something odd. There were several tops of heads poking out of the water at the cave entrance. I looked around and noticed that everyone was distracted. One of the agents hopped out of the water and moved behind a pillar that was helping to hold up the cave. It appeared that he had an automatic gun so I knew that there was going to be some sort of shoot out.

I walked away in the other direction to hide behind the couch in the living room. On the other side of the base, I heard all thirty-five of the agents started to climb out of the water. I saw Nova as she stayed in the backline of the troops while she was making her way over to me.

I saw the flashes of guns fire and all of a sudden, people started to drop like flies. There was so much going on, everything I was watching seemed to slow down, as if I was watching it in slow motion. Nova made it over to me and by that point five of our agents were wounded and had fallen to the ground.

I asked Nova, "Are you okay?"

She said, "Yes, I've been worried sick about you Kane. I thought you were a goner. I kept on running once I saw him throw you in the trunk. It was a long run back and by the time I made it back, it was too late for them to try to go back and save you. We went out on a mission as we tracked your location through the tracking device. We had to wait for the right moment and make sure you weren't moving around so we could come to rescue you."

I cut her off, "I'm so glad your okay Nova," as I hugged her.

She pulled a Glock out of her back pocket and said, "Use this for your own protection. Never use it unless you feel the need to."

I nodded my head as she showed me how to turn the safety on and off. She told me to stay put as she ran back into the madness to fight.

I watched her as she had a Glock in each of her hands pulling the triggers in a one, two, one, two pattern. I looked across the cave and I saw it with my own eyes. A man was aiming at Nova and in slow motion, I yelled, NOVA LOOK OUT!"

Chapter Eighteen

As her eyes made contact with mine, she was shot in the chest. She fell to her knees holding her chest. Her eyes never left mine as she fell face-first into the ground. I screamed, "Noooooooooooooo!"

I ran over to her, straight through the line of fire and pulled her body off to the side. The next thing I remember is getting shot three times. Once in the arm, shoulder and my left leg.

Everything went black and when I opened my eyes, I was in the hospital. No one was around me and everything was bright, as if I was looking directly into the sun without sunglasses on. I squinted my eyes as I was struggling to keep them open.

I turned my head to the right and saw a hospital bed with a body bag on it. The nurse came in and asked me how I was feeling.

I asked her who was in the body bag to the left and she said she goes by the name Nova. My eyes started to water as I knew I had just lost one of my best friends. The nurse said, "I'm going to contact your friends and family to let them know you're awake now."

"How long have I been asleep for?" I asked.

She responded, "Oh you've been in a coma for quite some time. I think tomorrow marks the third week. Nova just died around 15 minutes ago."

I started to cry as I realized I wouldn't be able to hug Nova again as she lay on her deathbed right next to me. I unzipped the bag to look at her face. A couple of my tears landed right on her cheek.

I said my goodbyes to Nova and stuck my bracelets on her wrist that I have had worn since as long as I could remember.

The doctor told me to sit back down and that I wasn't fully recovered yet. I got back in the bed and watched them wheel the bed with Nova out of the room. I knew that would be the last time I saw her as I continued to cry.

About an hour later, Agent 503 walked in and asked me how I was feeling. He told me how they captured most of the criminals in this scam and how Ma Parker was shot and killed. He also informed me that the US government had offered a reward for the return of the gold. 15 percent of the gold would be split between all of the agents involved in its recovery. The gold has been secured and it is soon getting moved out of the cave.

The following week I was released from the hospital and Agent 503 picked me up from the hospital. He told me they haven't started to move the gold yet because they were waiting for me. They brought a crane to Peter Pan Land and set it up so that they could pick up large boxes of gold from the water, moving it onto trucks.

There were one hundred or so workers helping to move the gold out from the cave. Each worker was searched at the end of their shift to make sure they weren't stealing any gold. To move the amount of gold that was stolen, it took a total of two weeks. Eventually the workers made their way to the last layer of gold.

We talked to an FBI agent who told Agent 503 and I that there would be around one hundred million dollars in gold for each of the agents who participated in the capture of this criminal organization. My mouth dropped and I started to think of all of the things I could buy with that money. I wouldn't have to pay for college and I could live off this money for the rest of my life. I could get a job and use that money as my own personal spending money and use eight million of the one hundred million to live the rest of my life. I could set aside the rest of the millions in case of some sort of emergency.

All of a sudden, one of the FBI agents called us over and said we needed to look at something. There was some sort of crate in the middle of the floor sticking out a little. We grabbed it by the handles and lifted it up. The crate had a lock on it and no one knew the combination. I told everyone to wait right where they were and I ran over to the couch, flipping it over.

Underneath the couch read a message, "You will see, once your eyes follow the opposite of me."

I thought to myself, by this point I'm almost a pro at cracking these riddles.

"Where could he be," I asked myself.

He's dead now so he's not anywhere. Unless he believes in the afterlife. I'm going to guess because he's a criminal than he's going to be in Hell. So, if the next clue is the opposite of him, it must be up. Agent 503 yelled, "What's the hold-up?"

I looked up at the ceiling and pointed. It was the combination to the lock. The combination read, "Have fun."

Agent 503 put the combination in and it opened. I ran over the crate and they pulled a scroll out of it. I looked at it as if it were two-hundred years old.

We started to unroll it. I looked at Agent 503 and he looked at me.

The scroll read, "Your luck just ran out. This is only a quarter of the gold. Have fun finding the rest. The other three locations are located among the shore of Lake Michigan."

On the bottom of the scroll read the first clue, "It's almost like a silver spoon keeps moving the sand."

I knew we were in for a great adventure figuring out the mystery of the stolen gold.

To be continued...

Favorite Quotes

"The difference between stupidity and genius is that genius has its limits."

– Albert Einstein

"The first time I sang in the church choir; two hundred people changed their religion."

– Fred Allen

"Have you ever noticed that anybody driving slower than you is an idiot, and anyone going faster than you is a maniac?"

– George Carlin

"Whoever said money can't buy happiness didn't know where to shop."

– Gertrude Stein

"I've got all the money I'll ever need, if I die by four o'clock."

– Henny Youngman

"People who think they know everything are a great annoyance to those of us who do."

– Isaac Asimov

"Money is not the most important thing in the world. Love is. Fortunately, I love money."

– Jackie Mason

Follow Instagram

@AuthorJamesFord

Made in the USA
Monee, IL
25 January 2020